Pop gave Moe a job.
"Get the rake and the
hoe," said Pop.

Moe got the rake and
the hoe.
"Take the rake and
make a big pile,"
said Pop.

Pop used the hoe to dig.
Moe used the rake.
Moe did not like to use
the rake.

Moe ran in to get a
red pen.
He sat on his bed.

Moe made a red line
on his toe.
"I can tie it up and
tape it," said Moe.

Pop did not see Moe.
Pop came in to get him.

"I can not rake,"
said Moe.
"See my big toe,"
said Moe.
"It has a big cut on it."

Pop saw the red line,
and he saw it was not
a cut.

"It is sad," said Pop.
"Moe can not get up,
and Mom has made
a big lime pie."

"Lie on the bed,"
said Pop.
"It is a bad cut."

"A pie!" said Moe.
"I am fine. See my toe,"
said Moe.
"It is not cut."

"I do not like to rake,"
said Moe.
"So I made up a lie."

"I see," said Pop.
"It is not like you
to lie. Time to get the
rake, Moe," said Pop.

Moe got the rake and
made a big pile.
Moe did a fine job.

It got late.
Moe ran in to see Pop
and Mom.
"I did my job," said Moe.

Pop was not mad at him.
Mom gave him pie.
Moe had a fine time.